To my ...
Ke...

Johnny Plowboy

By

Loran D. Wimbish,
with Ken Wimbish

© 2002 by Loran D. Wimbish, with Ken Wimbish. All rights reserved.

No part of this book may be reproduced, stored in a retrieval system, or transmitted by any means, electronic, mechanical, photocopying, recording, or otherwise, without written permission from the author.

ISBN: 1-4033-7302-7 (e-book)
ISBN: 1-4033-7303-5 (Paperback)

This book is printed on acid free paper.

1stBooks - rev. 11/15/02

"In the next great revival, God may not use a famous preacher or skilled orator to lead the movement. He may choose to use little Johnny Plowboy".

iv

TABLE OF CONTENTS

INTRODUCTION vii

CHAPTER ONE 1

CHAPTER TWO 4

CHAPTER THREE 9

CHAPTER FOUR 13

CHAPTER FIVE 19

CHAPTER SIX 22

CHAPTER SEVEN 27

CHAPTER EIGHT 31

CHAPTER NINE 36

CHAPTER TEN 46

CHAPTER ELEVEN 48

CHAPTER TWELVE 52

CHAPTER THIRTEEN 59

CHAPTER FOURTEEN 64

CHAPTER FIFTEEN 68

CHAPTER SIXTEEN 74

CHAPTER SEVENTEEN 82

CHAPTER EIGHTEEN 89

CHAPTER NINETEEN 96

CHAPTER TWENTY 100

CHAPTER TWENTY-ONE 106

CHAPTER TWENTY-TWO 110

CHAPTER TWENTY-THREE 116

CHAPTER TWENTY-FOUR 122

CHAPTER TWENTY-FIVE 126

Epilogue 134

ABOUT THE AUTHOR: *Loran Daniel Wimbish* 137

ABOUT THE AUTHOR: *Kenneth Wayne Wimbish* 138

INTRODUCTION

I have wanted to write this book for a long time, not because there are famous people or historic events to fill it, but to record some of my family's history. Indeed, my desire is greater to write our story than it is to write the story of someone of wealth, fame or prominence. Kipling wrote of not losing "the common touch", and I believe that the life of a common man can show us something of value. Those who follow us may profit from something we said or did or lived through; that would be my hope.

Although the desire to write the story had been with me for a long time, the actual execution of the project only became possible in the last couple of years. Through a wonderfully marvelous series of events, God brought me from California to Missouri and sat me down, literally, at my dad's kitchen table, where this book began to take shape and come into being.

The journey of many miles to get here was unimportant compared to the great journey down the corridors of my memory. People and events from the past came sweeping back as I worked through the story that my dad wrote down by hand. More thrilling yet was the journey through *his* memory, as he detailed things that happened before my birth, things that I wish I had been there to witness, things that I was being allowed to witness vicariously—thrilling things!

My dad always believed that God could and would use ordinary people to do His extraordinary business with humankind. You will see in these pages the great way God moved through an Oklahoma farm boy who came from a family of sharecroppers, a boy who, though poor, uneducated and without social prominence, was an eyewitness to the power of God to change lives for all eternity.

—Ken Wimbish

Johnny Plowboy

CHAPTER ONE

I write not as a well-known, ordained preacher of the gospel, but as a humble servant of Jesus Christ, God's Son and our Lord and Savior, Who gave His life that we might have life, and that more abundantly.

Two passages of Scripture, Galatians 1:10-12 and John 7:17, are very real to me. I believe that God has used them in my life as mainstays. Although I would make no attempt to compare myself with the formally educated and very wise Apostle Paul, I will say with him

Loran D. Wimbish, with Ken Wimbish

"That the gospel which was preached by me...I neither received from man, nor was I taught it, but it came through the revelation of Jesus Christ".

"If anyone wills to do His will, he shall know concerning the doctrine, whether it is from God..." (John 7:17). This scripture was certainly a mainstay for me; it rescued me from darkness and brought me into His marvelous light. I took that verse literally, and came to believe that no one could lead me astray if only I would do the will of God. The confidence I had in this scripture, and the assurance it

Johnny Plowboy

brought me, came from God, and was not of myself.

Then, too, to help make my life what it is today, God gave me a precious little Holiness girl. She sacrificed a more comfortable and perhaps more enjoyable life to join with me in marriage. We have now had fifty-eight years together, and I am more convinced than ever that God used her to help shape my life and ministry. I would not be what I am today without God or without His precious gift of her in my life.

God gave us four wonderful children, three boys and a girl. I pray for them every day that

Loran D. Wimbish, with Ken Wimbish

they will join their mother and me around the Throne Eternal when we all have ceased from this life.

CHAPTER TWO

I was born April 28, 1921, in the little East-Central Oklahoma town of Cowlington, population 250. It was off the beaten path, to be sure. I was the third of ten children. We were poor tenant farmers.

When I married and left home at age 22, we were still farming with horse-drawn implements that we would walk behind,

Johnny Plowboy

holding the handles. We never had an implement with a seat on it. We would walk in soft, turned soil behind a plow or cultivator along a quarter-mile row, often totaling thirty miles on those long summer days. Now there's a way to keep your weight down!

In the twenty-two years I was at home before I left to marry, we never owned a car or any piece of motorized farm equipment.

Electricity and propane gas were not available in our area. We cooked and heated the house with wood, and used kerosene lamps for light. We drew water out of a well with rope and bucket. My mother did laundry under

Loran D. Wimbish, with Ken Wimbish

an oak tree, scrubbing the clothes on a rub board and boiling them in a black wash kettle over an open fire.

I did very poorly in school. Our school went only through the eighth grade. I had already passed my seventeenth birthday when I finally got out of the eighth grade.

I was draft age when World War II began. However, I failed the physical examination at the induction center, and was told that I was not physically fit for military service. They sent me home.

During the last half of my teen years, our country was in what is known as the Great

Johnny Plowboy

Depression of the Thirties and early Forties. I see pictures in the encyclopedia, and read articles there of the drought and the great dust storms—I lived through that. I saw those dust storms that so hid the sun that chickens would go to roost, as though night had come.

The stock market crash in 1929, coupled with the drought, made for very difficult times indeed. As I reflect on those times, I am unsure even now what we did and how we made it, but we did make it. I have made it, in fact, to the age of eighty-one; I have a comfortable house, warm in winter and cool in summer; a good, dependable vehicle to drive; and weekly

Loran D. Wimbish, with Ken Wimbish

fellowship with God's wonderful people in church. Truly, God's blessings are rich, and He adds no sorrow with them (Proverbs 10:22).

Johnny Plowboy

CHAPTER THREE

I mentioned that it is difficult to recall exactly how we made it through the most trying of these times. One particular year, which was maybe the worst year of that period of time, I will describe as best I can.

We always raised most of what we ate. For example, we never bought bread out of a store; my Mom baked all the bread we ate. We usually had biscuits for breakfast, and cornbread for dinner and supper. Most of the time, we made the biscuits from flour bought

Loran D. Wimbish, with Ken Wimbish

from the store. A fifty-pound sack of flour cost, at that time, about fifty cents. But getting the fifty cents was the problem, and we did not always manage that. So we sometimes had cornbread for breakfast.

Our cornbread was made from meal ground at the local grist mill from corn raised on the farm. The man running the grist mill would take a toll, or a small portion, out of the corn as his pay for grinding our corn into meal for us.

Let me relate a humorous incident that happened to me. One day my Dad asked me to take a turn of corn to the mill, since Mom was almost out of meal. When I got the corn

Johnny Plowboy

shelled up, the sack was too much for me to carry, and it was quite a distance to the mill. No team or wagon was on hand to use. We had a horse colt, about two years old, running in the pasture. He was very gentle, but had not been broken to work or to ride, and he had never been off the place. I figured he was so gentle, he would not be much of a problem.

I put the sack of corn on him, then got on myself and headed for the mill. The colt got to wanting to turn around and go back home. I insisted he take me and my sack of corn on to the mill. He won! He just pitched me and my

Loran D. Wimbish, with Ken Wimbish

sack of corn off, and went back home. So much for that.

Johnny Plowboy

CHAPTER FOUR

In that worst year of the depression, we experienced complete crop failure. Our two main crops were cotton and corn, the cotton being our cash crop. When we picked it, we hauled it away to the cotton gin and sold it. For many years, that was our only source of income, in terms of actual money. The corn crop was for feeding our livestock and for making our bread.

In the Fall of the year, when the corn was ready for the harvest, we would take a wagon

Loran D. Wimbish, with Ken Wimbish

to the field and hand pick the corn. Then we took it to the barn, stored it for use all the way through to the next harvest. But this particular year was different—we didn't need a wagon.

My Dad took what we called a tow sack, also called a gunney sack, which was a burlap bag made to hold about a hundred pounds of potatoes. He walked the entire field, then came back with the sack half full. And there was not a good ear in the bunch, just little, underdeveloped ears that we called "nubbins".

As he put that half-sack of nubbins in the barn, he said "That's it". The problem was, we had a year ahead of us during which we would

Johnny Plowboy

have to feed the work mules, feed a couple of milk cows, fatten a few hogs for our meat supply, feed the chickens, and make our bread. We couldn't go to a neighbor to buy corn; we didn't have any money and they didn't have any corn.

I do not remember what we did, or how we got by. The land-lord received no rent that year, as we were sharecroppers with no crop to share.

* * * *

We did have somewhat of an alternative, though, in gathering some of the wild things that grew. These wild fruits, nuts and greens

Loran D. Wimbish, with Ken Wimbish

seemed to do a little better, in those lean years, than the things we had planted and cultivated. The wild fruits consisted of blackberries, which were plentiful for such a time as it was; wild plums, very delicious; some wild grapes and quite a lot of wild cherries; and huckleberries, a very tasty fruit. There was also something we called "haws". In our area, there were both black haws and red haws, and we liked them very much.

As for the nuts, we could find black walnuts, hickory nuts and quite a few native pecans. Sometimes I would go to the woods, sit under a hickory nut tree, crack the nuts on a

Johnny Plowboy

rock and eat them. I remember that we gathered and stored them in sacks so that, in the winter, we could sit and crack them on the large stone hearth of the old fireplace.

The wild greens consisted mostly of what we called "polk", also called polk greens or polk salad. We used it most freely in season, and canned it for use during the rest of the year.

Let me say something here about those long, hot and toilsome days in the fields. I have mentioned that we had no modern machinery or motorized equipment on the farm. Even though the work was very tiresome at times, I

Loran D. Wimbish, with Ken Wimbish

do not remember that there was a lot of stress, such as is noticeable today. People seem so stressed out now. I don't remember having that kind of stress in those days, even though the times were hard and so was the work.

Maybe part of the answer is in the humorous statement that reminds us of all the time-saving gadgets we have now. We have gadgets to do everything except our worrying. These time-saving gadgets give us—but of course—more time in which to worry.

Johnny Plowboy

CHAPTER FIVE

I was one of those who could perhaps be called the "heel" of the community, and even of the family. I know some members of the family might not think it was all that bad for me, but it hasn't been too far back that some of my brothers and sisters were talking and laughing in my presence about some of the dumb things I did and said when we were growing up.

I had almost no friends in school; it seems I was a loner. I was a natural-born coward. I can

Loran D. Wimbish, with Ken Wimbish

remember a few times when boys would chase me home from school, meaning to do me harm. I ran as hard as I could to get away from them. It did no good for me to try to stand my ground, because others would assist against me, and I didn't have a chance. I was actually afraid to go to school, but I had to go anyway.

I can truly say there is nothing in my heart against anyone for anything that was said or done that hurt me. God has taken care of all that. The truth is, things have really turned around for me, and I have many, many wonderful friends. God is so good!

Johnny Plowboy

Recently, some have said to me that they doubted that I had an enemy in the world. I know the Bible says to beware when all men speak well of you, but the pendulum does swing from one extreme to the other.

You may think that I say negative things about myself. That may be. One thing I've always said: I'm glad the Lord loves me as much as He does smart people.

Loran D. Wimbish, with Ken Wimbish

CHAPTER SIX

Now I am going to turn my attention to the best part of my life. This best part began in 1938. I was seventeen years old. We were in the middle of the Great Depression. It was the year I got saved.

Even though there was a Bible in our home all my life, I knew almost nothing about it. At the time of my conversion, I didn't even know the difference between the Old Testament and the New Testament. But my heart was hungry

Johnny Plowboy

for reality. I did not know that reality could be found only in Christ.

I was not going to church. In that little town where I was born and raised, there were three churches: Methodist, Baptist and Church of Christ. I had no knowledge of Pentecostal people.

One day I was walking along the street— really just a dirt road running between the stores of our little town—and I passed by two people who were just standing and talking. I don't remember who they were. I didn't stop or take notice of them, and they paid no attention to me. But I overheard one say to the other,

Loran D. Wimbish, with Ken Wimbish

"There is an old-fashioned revival meeting going on over at Cooper Hill". That was a community three and a half miles from our home west of town. It was indeed just a hill—no store, school house or post office.

At the time, I really did not know just what an old-fashioned revival meeting was. But I do remember that when those words fell upon my ears, something happened to me. That "something", I can't explain, and don't understand. An old saying I used to hear may come near to explaining it: something just turned over in my soul.

Johnny Plowboy

I'm not saying that that was the moment of my conversion. But whatever it was that happened to me caused me to make up my mind that I would go to that place, that revival meeting. I would just see what was going on over there.

I had no transportation other than to walk. I was plenty used to that. I walked there that evening, got there early, and found a brush arbor. I would see a number of them after that.A brush arbor was a simple structure consisting of a few standing poles, some smaller poles across the top of them, and brush piled on top of that. The dried leaves of the

Loran D. Wimbish, with Ken Wimbish

brush would make a rustling sound whenever the wind stirred them.

I got there well ahead of service time; not many had gathered yet. I sat down on a rock across the road, just looking at that old arbor. The late-afternoon breeze rustled through the leaves, and to this hungry-hearted, lonely boy, it seemed like those leaves were gently praising the Lord.

Soon others came, and they began lighting kerosene lanterns and hanging them on the arbor posts and nearby trees. There was no electricity. The seats were rough-sawn boards laid across stumps and rocks.

Johnny Plowboy

CHAPTER SEVEN

When they began to sing and praise the Lord, it was wonderful indeed. I had never seen such happy, joyous people—and remember that this was in the midst of the Great Depression. I immediately became so hungry for what they had. I wanted to join that happy band, and on to glory go.

That series of meetings lasted five and a half weeks. They had a water baptismal service, in a farm pond, about halfway through

Loran D. Wimbish, with Ken Wimbish

the revival, and had another at the end of the revival.

One night, my heart broke so that I went to the altar. I had never wept so in my life. The Lord graciously saved me. When my sin burden rolled away, I knew that I was completely forgiven of all my past. I had never experienced anything like that in my life. I felt so clean. As a babe in Christ, I had a lot to learn, and He is still working on me, but what a glorious day that was when He washed my sins away. Thanks be unto God for His unspeakable gift (II Corinthians 9:15).

Johnny Plowboy

There was a little log church house at the place where the old brush arbor was located. That little log church was my first home church, and my first pastor was a full-blood Choctaw Indian woman. In our area were many Indians, as it was a part of what had been the old Choctaw Indian Reservation. Both Choctaw and English were spoken in the area.

The log church has a history that goes back actually before I was born. I don't know that there is anything on record anywhere of what I'll relate here. Much of this story must necessarily be from my memory of the stories told to me, since the story begins before my

Loran D. Wimbish, with Ken Wimbish

birth. Most of what I will relate came to me from the pastor personally. I will tell the story as she told me, from the best of my memory and without adding to that.

Johnny Plowboy

CHAPTER EIGHT

About 1917 a preacher came down through that part of Oklahoma preaching revivals. He would preach in what we called store-front buildings, or in school houses, tents or brush arbors. The communities where he preached all had names, although sometimes we didn't know how a name came to be. They were places like Tucker, Short Mountain, Flower Hill, Bell Point, Jingle Ridge, Star, Blaine Bottom, Red Hill, Rockford, Harper, Lone Dove and my birthplace, Cowlington. I have

Loran D. Wimbish, with Ken Wimbish

been to all these communities at one time or another. These communities had schools, which were two to four rooms in size.

The preacher came to our area to hold a revival in a community we called Quinine Flat. His kind of preaching was new to us; he was a pentecostal preacher. He used terms that were unfamiliar to us: "know-so salvation" and "heart-felt religion". Most folks thought you could not know you were saved; you could only hope for the best and, when you got to Heaven, see if they would let you in. The "heart-felt religion" they identified as

Johnny Plowboy

emotionalism, thinking it had nothing to do with salvation.

As he preached, he would assure the people that if they would come to the altar, believe and obey the Scripture he preached, God would confirm the truth of the Scripture. God would save them from their sin, give them a new life, and they could have a 'know-so salvation". Many responded to the preaching, and God did confirm His word.

The preacher had another message, too. "Have you heard yet that God is pouring out His Spirit again as He did in the Book of Acts? Have you heard yet that people are being

Loran D. Wimbish, with Ken Wimbish

baptized in the Holy Ghost, and speaking in other tongues, just as back then?" We had not heard that yet.

Again he would say, "If you will come to the altar, believe and obey the Scripture that I have preached to you, God will confirm that I have preached to you the truth. He will baptize you in the Holy Ghost". Again, many responded, and again, God confirmed His word.

He had yet another message that he preached—miraculous Divine healing for the physical body, as in the Book of Acts, and deliverance from bondages. Again the

Johnny Plowboy

instructions: If you will come, believing and obeying the Scriptures, God will confirm His Word by healing and delivering you. And again the response: people were coming forward for prayer, and God did confirm His Word by healing, delivering and doing many miraculous things, things that have no human explanation. They knew God was at work.

Loran D. Wimbish, with Ken Wimbish

CHAPTER NINE

I have mentioned earlier an old pentecostal pioneer. I want to tell you about another one that I also got to hear in his older years, before he passed on. When he was just a single boy still living at home, some people came to their community and held a revival. It may have been the first pentecostal revival there.

The boy's family was a farming family. They attended the revival, and the whole family was saved, and accepted the pentecostal way. One day soon after, this boy was plowing

Johnny Plowboy

in a field. His dad came across the field to see how he was doing.

I can well identify with that scene. I grew up as one of ten children, and sometimes we would be scattered across the farm, some plowing in one field, some hoeing in another, and so forth. I remember my Dad making the rounds, checking on the work and seeing how we were doing.

(I remember times of being in the field at about the dinner hour. We did not have a dinner bell, so Mom would take a plowshare in one hand and a hammer in the other—that was our call to the dinner table).

Loran D. Wimbish, with Ken Wimbish

Back to the boy: When the dad came up to the boy as he plowed, he saw that the boy was crying.

"What's the matter, son?" the dad asked.

"Dad, God has called me to preach".

The dad bowed his head and stood quietly for a while. Then he raised his head.

"Well, son, if God has called you to preach, you'd better go on and obey Him. Give me the lines".

The boy handed over the lines that guided the team of horses. The dad put the lines across his shoulders, stepped between the plow

Johnny Plowboy

handles and clucked to the team. "You go on and obey the Lord".

The boy walked off the field, and began right away to go from community to community, preaching revivals. He preached in storefronts, which were usually-vacant store buildings, and in schoolhouses, tents and brush arbors. He had a long and fruitful ministry. I heard it said that a church was established almost every place where he preached a revival, and that in time, you could trace his trail by the churches that were established as he crisscrossed the state of Oklahoma.

Loran D. Wimbish, with Ken Wimbish

I recall a time, when I was quite a young man, I was in a meeting where that man was present. They asked the feeble old fellow to take the pulpit, and I got to hear him preach.

I recently heard the humorous story about a boy plowing in a field with his mule. He saw a cloud overhead, and in the cloud he could make out the letters "GP". He just knew that stood for "go preach". He discussed it with his pastor, who wasn't sure the boy was cut out for preaching.

"Son", he counseled, "did you ever stop to think those letters might stand for "go plow"?

Johnny Plowboy

Of course, God can and does call people out of cornfields, or anywhere else, and put them in the ministry. With the cooperation and dedication of the individual, He can do as He chooses. We have what we have today because of some of the old-timers who gave it their best. Thank God for them.

I recall the Bible account of Elijah and Elisha. Elisha was plowing in his field when Elijah came by. Elijah threw his mantle over Elisha, who responded "Let me bid my father and mother goodbye, and I will follow you." Elisha then killed the oxen, boiled their flesh over a fire built with the wooden farming

Loran D. Wimbish, with Ken Wimbish

implements, served the meat to his neighbors in a fare-well dinner, and left, following Elijah.

At Bethel and Jericho, the sons of the prophets, who I understand to have been theology students, tried to get Elisha to stop off with them instead of following Elijah. "Don't you know that your master will be taken from you today?" they asked.

"Yes, I know. Hold your peace," answered Elisha, continuing to follow Elijah.

When they came to the Jordan River, Elijah stretched his mantle out over the water, and the water parted. They crossed on dry ground.

Johnny Plowboy

"What do you want from me, Elisha?" Elisha didn't say, I want to be able to preach like you. If that's what he had wanted, he could have stopped with the sons of the prophets and accomplished that.

But he said, "I want what you have, and a double portion of it".

"That is a hard thing to ask, but if you see me when I am taken away, it will be so", Elijah said.

As they went on, a whirlwind and chariots of fire swept Elijah away to heaven. His mantle fell to the ground. Elisha picked it up and started back toward the river.

Loran D. Wimbish, with Ken Wimbish

I have imagined Elisha waving the mantle and saying, "I've got it!" I can picture someone saying, "You've got what?"

Elisha replies, "I've got what that old man Elijah had".

"Oh, you have?"

Waving the mantle, Elisha could have replied, "Yes, don't you see it?"

But anyone could have picked up the mantle and waved it. The sons of the prophets weren't impressed with his waving of that mantle.

They said, "Let's go down to the river and see what happens when he gets there. That's

Johnny Plowboy

where we'll find out whether he has what the old man had or not".

When Elisha reached the river, he waved the mantle and said, "Where is the Lord God of Elijah"? Of course, the Lord God of Elijah was right there. The waters parted, and Elisha went across on dry land. The sons of the prophets could only say, "He's got it!"

The world—even the nominal church world—looks at us Pentecostals and listens to us say, we've got it. They're not too impressed, but they do want to know if it works. The real thing works. A good pattern to check it by is the Book of Acts in the Bible.

Loran D. Wimbish, with Ken Wimbish

CHAPTER TEN

I have heard lots of explanations of what revival really is. I will add my two cents worth. I see revival as bringing about something that has been renewed, restored to it's original condition.

There are people who like to restore vintage automobiles. Some are satisfied to restore just the outside of the old car, so that it looks real. They then do whatever they want inside, and under the hood. I remember a Ford Model T that had been restored just on the outside, but

Johnny Plowboy

the owner had put a souped-up engine and drive train in it. MY! You never saw a Model T scat like that one.

It was not, though, a real Model T; it just looked like one. It had not been restored to it's original condition. These days, some people don't even look like the real thing, let alone have inside that which is genuine. During the first half of the twentieth century, the "real thing" took the message of the Gospel across this nation like a wildfire.

Loran D. Wimbish, with Ken Wimbish

CHAPTER ELEVEN

That fire seemed to spread fastest during the Great Depression and the years of drought—most of the Thirties and some of the Forties. Millions of Americans were left jobless and homeless. Oklahoma suffered mightily. Blistering heat was almost unbearable. In July, 1934, new record temperatures were set daily. Those records still stand, in large part.

Johnny Plowboy

In one place, the temperature exceeded 100 degrees for thirty-six days in a row, the thirty-sixth day of that stretch reaching 117 degrees.

Farm closures were daily events. The farm we were renting in the early Thirties was a 60-acre farm. It had pasture and farm land, house, barn, chicken house and smokehouse. It sold for $1,000. There was no way we could afford to buy it, and since the man who bought it wanted to live there, we had to move. We moved to a farm that was owned by a loan company. They had foreclosed on it. More than one fourth of Oklahoma farmers wound up on welfare.

Loran D. Wimbish, with Ken Wimbish

Occasionally, the government would send a big truck loaded with food through the community. They would send information ahead of time about the time and place of arrival of what we called the commodity wagon. People would be lined up there. Food was handed out according to the number of people in the family.

During a few short years, the population of the state of Oklahoma declined by about a million people. Many went elsewhere to try to find work to support their families; quite a few of those went to California.

Johnny Plowboy

Some of our relatives, and many others we knew, went to California during those years, and never returned. Some are still alive, and still there. Our family never left; we stuck it out, the Lord only knows how. I stuck it out, an individual nineteen years old.

I remember my mother making me a shirt out of an old, worn-out cotton sack. I don't know that she even had a pattern to go by. She just cut it out and sewed it up. No buttons to put on it—she just pinned up the front with two big safety pins. I wore that thing to school, what little I went, that winter.

Loran D. Wimbish, with Ken Wimbish

CHAPTER TWELVE

I have previously mentioned the Assemblies of God organization. At the beginning of the Great Depression and the drought years, they listed 110 churches. By 1939, they listed 394 churches, a growth rate of 358 per cent in a decade or less. Think of that—the greatest growth during the greatest depression.

Let me give one more testimony of the outstandingly miraculous. When we were just married, in 1943, I was invited to preach in a

Johnny Plowboy

little country church at Vassar, in north-central Oklahoma. The pastor was a woman. Her husband was not a preacher, but was a good Christian man who fully supported and helped in the ministry of his wife. He was a farmer; their name was Stewart. Their son, Verlin Stewart, was a long-time Assemblies of God missionary to Colombia.

I don't remember that I was ever in a more godly home, where the presence of the Lord was more rich and real. What a family! I still cherish the thoughts of that time, now fifty-six years past.

Loran D. Wimbish, with Ken Wimbish

Sister Stewart was at that time an elderly woman, at least viewed from my young vantage point. I referred to her as Mother Stewart. As I always enjoyed testimonies about things that had happened to older folks in their early ministries, I asked her one day, "Mother Stewart, choose a testimony from the early days of your pioneer ministry, and relate it to me".

"All right", she said. "I will tell you about the time of a great flu epidemic, one you have probably heard about". I had indeed heard my parents talk of the same.

Johnny Plowboy

She continued, "During that flu epidemic, I was pastoring a little country church, and my husband was farming. We had no motor vehicle. We farmed with teams of horses or mules." This was in north-central Oklahoma, and the winters can be pretty rough there.

"One winter night", she said, "there was a winter storm on—lots of snow and sleet. In the wee hours of the morning, the old wall telephone rang." Her family was all down with the flu. She herself was affected, but was the only one able to get up and care for the rest of the family.

Loran D. Wimbish, with Ken Wimbish

She answered the phone, then returned to bed weeping. Her husband asked her what the phone call was about, and why she was crying. She told him that it was one of the faithful families of the church. They were all down with the flu, and would it be possible, they wondered, for the pastor to get to them, through the storm, and pray for them. She had had to tell them of her own family's illness, and that, because of the illness and the weather, she could not come to them.

Her husband said, "You, as their pastor, are the only shepherd they have. I believe we should try to get to them, or die on the way."

Johnny Plowboy

He had not been getting up for anything, but he got up, dressed himself, lit a kerosene lantern and told her to prepare the children. He went out into the winter night, harnessed a team, hitched them to a wagon and drove to the front of the house. She had the children all wrapped up in bundles of blankets and quilts.

They put the children into the wagon, and set out for the home of the other family. There, they carried the bundled-up children in, laid them on the floor and began to pray. Pretty soon, one of the children began to kick around, got out of the bundle of blankets, stood up and asked for something to eat. They found the

Loran D. Wimbish, with Ken Wimbish

child to be well. They praised the Lord, and prayed on.

By the time daylight came, every member of both families had been healed. They had an old-fashioned country fellowship breakfast. After that, they returned to their home, and were not bothered by the flu anymore.

I realize how foolish such things look. Taking a sick family out on a winter night, to a home where there is yet more sickness—this is not ordinary thinking. What imposing circumstances! I sometimes wonder, though, how many great blessings we miss by looking at circumstances.

Johnny Plowboy

CHAPTER THIRTEEN

I can believe easily enough in God's miracles, because I have witnessed some such myself, even in my own body. One night, during the revival at Quinine Flat, the preacher was working at the altar, which was filled with people who had responded to the call. As he was working along the altar, he came to an Indian woman who was just sitting on the altar.

He said to her, "Would you like to be saved?" She replied that she would like to be saved, but she was too sinful and too far gone.

Loran D. Wimbish, with Ken Wimbish

"God would never save a creature like me". She told the preacher that she was bound by tobacco and alcohol, and was so diseased that she was in constant pain and misery, suffering day and night without relief.

(After I grew up, and became acquainted with her, I heard her talk about this. Her own description of her condition left me with the impression that her flesh was almost rotting off her bones.)

She told the preacher that even though she didn't believe God would save her, she knew that some of those people had been healed— including some people that she knew doctors

Johnny Plowboy

could not help. She knew that it was God who had healed them.

She said to the preacher, "I just came to the altar to see if you kind white people would put your hands on me and pray for me. Maybe God will give me a little relief from this awful, constant pain and suffering.

"Yes, we will pray for you," said the preacher. He put his hand on her and started to pray. She toppled off the altar onto the ground.

Sometimes there was sawdust on the ground under those brush arbors. Hence the term "down the sawdust trail" or "walk the sawdust trail" to describe those walking

Loran D. Wimbish, with Ken Wimbish

forward to the altar to be saved. Many times, though, there was no sawdust, only dirt. Such was the case under the brush arbor where I was saved: no sawdust. As I write these words, my soul is overflowing with the joy that began sixty-four years ago when, as a seventeen-year-old boy, I walked a drought-dusty dirt trail to the altar.

Onto that same kind of dirt floor toppled the old Indian woman. The Christians gathered around her to pray as she rolled and tossed about. The devil does all he can, always, to keep his hold on someone, and a great struggle was on. The hot weather, the dusty floor, the

Johnny Plowboy

perspiring body, the diseased flesh and the overpowering stench of one long addicted to tobacco and alcohol combined to overwhelm those standing nearby. The smell was awful, it was said.

Before the night was gone, the struggle was over. She had been saved, sanctified, baptized in the Holy Ghost, healed—made completely whole. She was also called into ministry, as I shall relate now.

Loran D. Wimbish, with Ken Wimbish

CHAPTER FOURTEEN

The revival finally closed and the preacher moved on. A good number of people had been saved and healed, and had embraced the pentecostal doctrine. But at that time, 1917, there was no pentecostal church in that area for those dear people to attend. The old-line denominational churches disowned those who became pentecostal, and did not welcome them back into fellowship.

This new pentecostal group did not even know where to look for a pentecostal preacher

Johnny Plowboy

to pastor them. They just held what are called "cottage prayer meetings". They were praying and talking together, trying to come up with someone who would pastor them and help them establish a church.

One day, as they were discussing the matter, the Indian woman who had had such a marvelous miracle said, "Someone has to do something". She had no formal education, and could not even read or write her own name. "If you people will help me learn to read", she offered, "I'll get me a Bible and try to help this community in this way, God being my helper".

Loran D. Wimbish, with Ken Wimbish

She did learn to read, and did become the leader of the group.

After she had her great and glorious experience with the Lord, and He had delivered her from the foulness of her sinful, addicted life, she started wearing white clothing only. So far as I know, and I knew her for several years after I grew up, she never again wore anything other than white. Once someone asked her if she thought it was a sin to wear other than white clothes.

"No," she replied, "but I was so dirty and filthy for so long. When God did what He did

Johnny Plowboy

for me, I wanted to wear only pure white, and

be reminded of the righteousness of God."

Loran D. Wimbish, with Ken Wimbish

CHAPTER FIFTEEN

Stories of the days when she was learning to read were still around when I was growing up. The stories came often from men who had been walking through the woods, looking for cattle, or taking shortcuts from place to place, or some such. They would find her, deep in the woods and deep in prayer, her Bible before her on a rock or stump. As the tears poured from her face, she would pray, "Lord, help me to read this book. I know it is your word, because it did in my life what that preacher said it

Johnny Plowboy

would do". She would pray for the people in the community who had not come to hear the preacher: "They'll need someone to read the Scriptures to them, and tell them 'He'll do it for you, too'". She would pray for those who did come and hear but did not respond: "They'll need to have the Scriptures read to them again, and again." She would pray for those who came, heard and responded: "They'll need to have the Scriptures read to them, and have someone urge them on, help them hold on, help them grow in the faith." Her commitment was simple: "Lord, if you will help me read this Bible, I will serve in this

Loran D. Wimbish, with Ken Wimbish

place. I will see that this community hears your word, and is given the opportunity to respond."

The time came when a church was formed, she became the pastor, and a building was started. People from the community cut trees from the nearby woods to build a log church house. The logs were not hewn to shape; they were just the rough logs straight from the woods. The chips that were chopped from the logs when they notched the corners were placed in the cracks between the logs, then the cracks were cemented. There was no siding outside, and no paneling inside. Outside or inside, you could see rough logs.

Johnny Plowboy

There was no electricity and no plumbing. All the labor was donated. I distinctly remember being told that there was less than one hundred dollars in actual money spent on the building.

The Indian woman, Sister Cornelia Cooper by name, had a tremendous ministry in the area. She was, for example, a great help to the pentecostal work in McCurtin, Oklahoma. There had been much difficulty in the several attempts to start a pentecostal church there. Sister Cooper was successful in getting them firmly established, and helped bring them into the Oklahoma District of The Assemblies of

Loran D. Wimbish, with Ken Wimbish

God. The little log church of which she became pastor came into that denomination, too, being listed in their yearbooks in the Thirties and Forties as the Cooper Hill Assembly of God.

Regardless of how good and holy a person is, there are always people who don't like that person, and who will speak all manner of evil. Of course, this dear lady was no exception. She came in for her share of criticism, and was the subject of gossip. This hurt me very badly, as I knew her well and had benefited from her ministry. She had been such a great help to me in my early Christian life.

Johnny Plowboy

To cite one example that is still very well in my memory: There was a man in the area that did not like pentecostal people. He spoke against her, and perhaps gave her trouble. He had lots of "friends" who were like himself.

There came a time when he became disabled, and could not take care of himself. No one was interested in helping him. The old Indian preacher woman built a little room across the road from her house, and brought the man there. She cared for him for the remainder of his life.

Loran D. Wimbish, with Ken Wimbish

CHAPTER SIXTEEN

Many things of significance came about in that log cabin church. People began to receive the baptism in the Holy Ghost just as in the Book of Acts. Many came, from far and near, to receive this baptism. It was said that no one who went there with the intention of receiving this gift went away empty.

One of my wife's uncles told me that he went by team and wagon to that church in those days, traveling from Spiro, Oklahoma.

Johnny Plowboy

That is a distance of eighteen miles. He was not disappointed.

Almost everyone had a vegetable garden and a potato patch, to help with the food supply. Pastor Cooper was no exception. Occasionally, we would have no less than a plague of potato bugs, which could destroy a potato patch in short order. There was usually no money to buy bug spray.

One year, the bugs were devastating the potatoes. Pastor Cooper went out to the patch one day and saw that the bugs had started in along the edge. She said that she knelt down in the rows and prayed. "The bugs just walked off

Loran D. Wimbish, with Ken Wimbish

up the hill like turkeys", was the way she expressed it. It is true that the bugs did not advance any farther.

When I told this to my dear old Mom, she said, "Now, you know that's not true." This was one of the things that made my heart ache. Even though I was young in the Lord and new to pentecost, I already believed that God could do anything.

These days of modern conveniences are different from those days back then. I walked the three-and-a-half miles to church, a seven-mile round trip. Sometimes, someone would ask me to spend Sunday afternoon with them,

Johnny Plowboy

but if I went home between the morning and evening services, that meant fourteen miles on the road for the day, all on foot.

I walked that three-and-a-half miles in the blazing sun of the depression-era drought, sometimes having to step off the road and rest under a shade tree before resuming my journey. I have also walked that road in winter, when ice was crackling on the trees. And I have been at church when a rainstorm came up. Caught without rain gear, I've walked the whole distance in pouring rain.

I will never forget one particular night in that little log church. They always had a

Loran D. Wimbish, with Ken Wimbish

regular service on Saturday night. All the churches I knew of had Saturday night service, and wouldn't have thought of it being otherwise. One winter Saturday night, at the end of the service, we went to the door and found about a foot of snow on the ground. Snow was still falling, and there I was, three-and-a-half miles from home, and on foot. I didn't ask anyone if I could stay with them, and no one asked me to stay. Each one fended for himself.

It would have been very difficult to get home, and I knew that, even if I got home, I could not make it back for Sunday school and

Johnny Plowboy

church the next morning. And I certainly did want to be there on Sunday. So I just hung around until everyone else was gone. I dragged one of the slatted pews up close to the wood stove. I lay on that pew, and burned on one side and froze on the other. I just kept turning over and over. During the night, I would add wood to the fire, and stir it once in a while. I don't remember that I slept a wink—what a miserable night! But, praise the Lord, I was there for Sunday school and church, and without breakfast, too.

The snow had stopped that morning, and after the service I made my way home. Some

Loran D. Wimbish, with Ken Wimbish

people, in spite of the weather, were in that Sunday morning service, and I was one of them. Church meant everything to me. Oh, just to be there with those precious people!

There were some times when I didn't get to go to church for a while, for various reasons. I remember one time that I had not been in church for a while. One day, I was plowing corn with mules and a walking cultivator. My heart was aching so badly just to fellowship with God's people, I got to crying. No one else was in that particular field, so I stopped the team and got down between two of those corn rows. I poured my heart out to the Lord, and

Johnny Plowboy

oh, how He met me there in the cornfield, and

how He refreshed my soul!

Loran D. Wimbish, with Ken Wimbish

CHAPTER SEVENTEEN

I previously mentioned that I have not been ordained to the ministry. But at a young age, I began doing some lay preaching, and was licensed to preach for several years. I have worked as a machinist all of my adult life, with over fifty years in that field. During that time, I have pastored five different little country churches an accumulated total of twelve years.

The first church I pastored was in the hills of Arkansas, in a community called Greasy Valley. If you ever drove over the dirt roads in

Johnny Plowboy

the rain, you'd know why the place was called Greasy Valley; it was slick. I was so happy there, living in the parsonage right beside the little church.

We had some wonderful revival meetings during our time there. One meeting was special to me, because the preacher was my first pastor, the Indian woman, who was still living, though very aged. I went to where she was living, got her and brought her to Arkansas to hold the meeting for me. She seemed so pleased to see me there, trying to do something for the Lord.

Loran D. Wimbish, with Ken Wimbish

She was also in attendance later on, when I preached a revival in Oklahoma at the two-room frame schoolhouse where I got my first day's education. Again, I went to get her, and brought her to visit the revival that I was preaching in that schoolhouse. She just beamed as I preached. The Lord gave us a wonderful revival there.

I remember especially one thing of importance that occurred during the course of the meeting. I preached one night on the baptism in the Holy Ghost. One of my Mom's very good lady friends was there, a Mrs. Herring. She was a good Baptist lady whose

Johnny Plowboy

children had been with me in the early grades at that very school.

I was nearing the end of the message, but had not yet started the altar call. She jumped out of her seat, and came running forward with her hands in the air. She was shouting, "That's the truth, so help me, and I'm going to have it". AND SHE GOT IT! She spent the rest of her life as a Sunday school teacher in a pentecostal church. Praise the Lord!

While we were still at Harmony Assembly of God in Greasy Valley, Arkansas, something amusing happened one day as I was coming home from work. I was yet a half mile from

Loran D. Wimbish, with Ken Wimbish

home when I saw our three-year-old son Ken pulling his little red wagon down the road. Of course, I stopped and picked him up for the ride back home. I asked him why he was there, and where he was going. He said, "Mom told me to".

When I got home, I told my wife that I had picked him up a half mile down the road. She said she had told him to go out and see if Daddy was coming. She didn't know that he had latched onto his little red wagon and taken off down the road, and wasn't going to stop until he found me.

Johnny Plowboy

We eventually left there, and have not lived in that area again. After several years of being away from there, I had not had contact with the Indian woman preacher. I regularly read the Pentecostal Evangel, the official weekly magazine of The Assemblies of God, and noted the column listing the ministers who had retired or passed on. One day as I read the listing, my eyes fell upon the name Cornelia F. Cooper. There she was, with the date of her ordination and of her passing. The tears came, although not really for her; I know she had a triumphant entry into yonder world. They were

Loran D. Wimbish, with Ken Wimbish

the tears of knowing she was gone and that the

world would, for me, be a little more lonely.

Johnny Plowboy

CHAPTER EIGHTEEN

There are many things in my life that turned out to be important events, even though I did not recognize at the time that God was working those things by His will and for His glory. I can look back now and see the hand of the Lord in all of my life.

Some of the things that happened to me, I kept to myself, not sharing them even with my own family. One such I will relate now. It happened when I was in my teen years.

Loran D. Wimbish, with Ken Wimbish

We lived, as it was termed, "way back in the sticks". Our only transportation was either by team and wagon, on horseback or on foot. It was very seldom indeed that everyone was gone from home at the same time, but on this occasion did find myself alone there. I do not remember the reason that everyone was gone that day.

My mother always had a vegetable garden, to help feed the family. She had a mole trap, to help control the moles that were always trying to destroy the garden. That trap was a spring-loaded device with six sharp, steel prongs. When the trap was set, it's legs were pushed

Johnny Plowboy

into the ground, across the opening of the molehill. It was pushed far enough down so that the trigger was right at ground level. As the mole rooted along and tripped the trigger, the prongs would go right through the ground into the mole.

I was attempting to set the trap, which by necessity had very strong springs. I either did not get the trigger well set, or I accidentally tripped it somehow. When it tripped, one of the sharp steel prongs went into my wrist. When I pulled it out, the blood just spurted out. I knew there was an important artery there, having heard about suicide attempts, and I knew from

Loran D. Wimbish, with Ken Wimbish

the way the blood was running that I had hit that artery. All this happened much quicker than I am able to write it or you are able to read it. I did everything I could to get the flow of blood stopped, to no avail; I knew I would not last long.

I listened for the sound of a wagon creaking and thumping over the old country road—they could usually be heard quite a way—but there were none to be heard. I thought if I could catch up a horse, I could ride for help, but there were none in sight. There was of course no telephone. I looked across the field toward the nearest neighbor, and thought of making a run

Johnny Plowboy

for help. Running, though, would make the heart pump the blood out even faster. I resigned myself to the realization that the end had come.

I leaned against the wall of the house, and waited for the end. I was near the door, so the family would find me easily when they returned home. It did not occur to me to write them a note of explanation. Can you imagine what it is like for a teenage boy to be facing death, all alone? I leaned against the rough-sawn, unpainted lumber that was the outside of our house, holding my wounded hand in the

Loran D. Wimbish, with Ken Wimbish

other, looking down at it. I cannot describe the loneliness I felt.

I did not know if there was really any life after death. I was not really sure there was a real God that had created all things, was eternally alive and seeing all that was taking place. I knew that if there was life after death, then some preparation should be made, but I did not know what to do, and there was no one to help me.

It occurred to me that if there was a true and eternally living God, He could hear me if I spoke to Him. I had no idea how He would respond, but I decided to try. I said, "If there is

Johnny Plowboy

a true and living God, and you are hearing and seeing me, would you let me know by stopping this blood." The instant I said that, the blood stopped as if it had been turned off at a faucet. It did not congeal, thicken, slow down and stop, it just simply stopped abruptly.

Some may say that it just happened to stop, but I have always believed, and still do today, that it didn't just happen. That day, that moment, I made contact with the God of the Ages, the eternal God that made this world and all that is in it. I am sure that on that day God heard, and responded to my crying heart and

Loran D. Wimbish, with Ken Wimbish

had mercy on me, and that I am alive today because of it.

I have always given God the praise, the honor and glory for that. What a precious friend He is indeed! I love Him, and have always believed that I owe Him my life.

CHAPTER NINETEEN

I would like to say another thing about the Indian woman preacher. I remember her coming over to the little town of Cowlington, where I was born, and holding a revival. The meeting was held in some peoples' front yard;

Johnny Plowboy

the front porch was used as the platform. The preacher traveled a good distance each night, in a Model T and on a road that provided quite a roundabout way.

As was very common in those days, they had a few flat tires in their traveling back and forth to and from the meeting. She mentioned that their tires were rather old and worn. There was a man in the area who had a General Merchandise store in the little town, and was also one of the big farmers of the area. I knew that man for all of his life; I have worked for him in his fields. I don't know that he ever got saved. I don't remember him ever going to

Loran D. Wimbish, with Ken Wimbish

church, even to the revival that Sister Cooper was holding in the town.

But he knew Sister Cooper, and always referred to her as his preacher. Somehow, he heard about the trouble she was having with her old, worn tires. He put a full set of new tires on that Model T Ford as a contribution to her ministry.

Another thing comes to mind. Sister Cooper was married to a man named Curby, who was also a full-blood Choctaw Indian. He drove her to the meetings in the Model T. He was not a full-fledged pentecostal believer. Sometimes he was a little amused at some of her stories of

Johnny Plowboy

how she trusted in the Lord and was helped by Him.

I remember her telling about the time they were driving along the road and lost control of the car. The car ran off the road, bumped into a tree, and lodged against it with the front wheels off the ground. Curby looked at her and said, "God almost didn't help you that time, did He!"

Loran D. Wimbish, with Ken Wimbish

CHAPTER TWENTY

I mentioned earlier that I am a lay preacher. I have never derived my full support from ministry. I have been privileged to have a part in a few revivals. I will mention a few of them here.

In the late Forties—more than fifty years ago at this writing—my wife and I were living in Fort Smith, Arkansas. Just over the state line into Oklahoma a short way was a little white frame church house. The sign over the door

Johnny Plowboy

read "Assembly of God church". It sat beside a country road.

We found out that it was abandoned; no services or Sunday school were being held. It was referred to, as it is said, as "a burned-over field". The building had not been vandalized, the door was not locked, and the pews and piano were still there. We did not find out whether anyone was in charge of the building or not.

Another young brother and his wife joined my wife and me, and we started a revival in that vacant building. For a week, it seemed hopeless and very dead. One night on our way

Loran D. Wimbish, with Ken Wimbish

back to Fort Smith after the service, the other brother's wife was very discouraged. "Let's not go back any more," she said. "We won't even have to let them know. Nobody is coming out, and nothing is going to happen".

I told her, "We may go back there tomorrow night and find a crowd, and find revival breaking out." She thought that was quite hilarious, but it did happen just that way.

We went back the next night, and there was a crowd. It had to be the Lord that brought them out. The glory of the Lord fell, several were saved, and some were filled with the Holy Ghost. Before the meeting came to a

Johnny Plowboy

close, more were saved—27 in all—and nine had received the Holy Ghost. At least two who were saved in that revival subsequently entered the ministry. The brethren who handled the official matters set the church in order, and it has never closed down.

My wife and I were recently through the area, and we drove by that old church. They are now in their third building, a nice brick church house and parsonage.

We held another revival near that same time at the South Fort Smith Assembly. We had an overwhelming move of God. Night after night, the altar was filled with people seeking God.

Loran D. Wimbish, with Ken Wimbish

I have always loved working at the altar. One night, I was working and praying with people at the altar, and I became very hot and sweaty; it was summertime, and the church had no air conditioning. I went to the door and stepped out onto the porch for some fresh air.

I saw that the yard was full of people. I asked someone close by if the people had been there all during the service. I was told, No, they had been coming all along. Some had heard and come; some had not heard but felt they ought to come, and did. One or two had just wrapped a robe around themselves, and

Johnny Plowboy

had come and stood in the yard. What a tremendous meeting indeed!

It was not great preaching that brought about such meetings; it was God's great blessing. He smiled upon us with unmerited favor. How I praise His name!

Loran D. Wimbish, with Ken Wimbish

CHAPTER TWENTY-ONE

I would like to mention a few outstanding and miraculous healings that we were privileged to witness. Early in our married life, we were in the church in Fort Smith. Our pastor was C. A. Lasater, an older man and a very godly one. I have heard him say to our congregation, "Folks, there are people here who have been saved three weeks now and haven't seen a miracle yet." One miracle that we did see involved Brother McGovern, a member of that church.

Johnny Plowboy

Brother McGovern had several children, and all the family were faithful to the church. He became sick, and eventually was completely paralyzed, confined to a bed and unable to help himself. Much prayer had been offered for him. Everyone thought that he was bed-ridden for life, and he had resigned himself to that, too. The church was caring for the family, as the wife could not hold down a job and see to her husband and the children as well.

The circumstance seemed hopeless. Brother McGovern told us that he wanted to attend one more service in our little church. He said that

Loran D. Wimbish, with Ken Wimbish

he did not expect us to get him to and from service regularly, but he wanted to be in attendance one more time if some of the brethren could get him there. He lived two blocks from the church; he wondered if he could be carried on some kind of stretcher that short distance.

The neighbor next door had an old Army folding cot. We borrowed the cot, and got him on it. By holding on to the wooden frame, several men could carry him. He was taken to the church, and placed down front by the altar on the right side. We were not at that time

Johnny Plowboy

holding a revival campaign or special healing services.

During the service, the building began to be filled with the presence of God and His shekinah glory. It was visible to all as a thin blue haze. As God's glory filled the place, someone spontaneously started a Jericho March around the room. As we marched, we sang "When The Saints Go Marching In". At that point, Brother McGovern got up off the cot, folded it up and marched around the room with the cot on his shoulder.

After the service, he walked home carrying the cot. He returned it to the neighbor from

Loran D. Wimbish, with Ken Wimbish

whom he had borrowed it, and thanked him for the use of the cot. Can you imagine what the neighbor thought when he answered the knock at the door and saw Brother McGovern standing there with the cot on his shoulder?

CHAPTER TWENTY-TWO

Another outstanding miracle that we witnessed was in the First Assembly of God in Russellville, Arkansas, a church pastored by Judge Lindsay. The divine healing message had been made so real to one woman in the congregation that she stood and went to the

Johnny Plowboy

platform. She approached the pulpit where Brother Lindsay was, holding in her arms a little boy. The boy appeared to be three or four years old, though he was actually nine. He had been born paralyzed. He was bent together almost into a ball, with his arms and legs folded and useless. He could not speak.

He seemed to have a good mind. His bright eyes were responsive, and he could nod his head in apparently intelligent communication.

Brother Lindsay prayed for the boy, with no obvious result. He stepped back a little, and looked at the boy. He reached into his pocket, pulled out a little pocket knife, and held it up

Loran D. Wimbish, with Ken Wimbish

for the boy to see. As he held it at about arm's length from the boy, he asked him if he'd like to have the knife. The boy nodded yes.

"If you'll reach out and get it, you can have it," said the preacher. The boy's hand and arm unfolded, and he reached out and simply swept the knife from Brother Lindsay's fingers.

The boy's mother let out a scream. As she started to let the boy down to the floor, his legs unfolded and straightened under him like the landing gear of an airplane. The boy came down on his feet, stood, and walked. What a blessing to witness such a miracle!

Johnny Plowboy

That was in the late 1940s. In recent years I related that testimony in our present home church in Neosho, Missouri. After the service, I was approached by Manuel Portugal, one of the brothers of Sheri Portugal of our congregation. He said that he had heard a man in Arkansas tell this same story, and that he had told it exactly as I had.

While I am still on the subject of miracles, I want to tell about one that occurred in our own home. When our oldest son Ken was eleven years old, he developed a bone infection in his left ankle. It required surgery and a 29-day hospitalization at William Newton Memorial

Loran D. Wimbish, with Ken Wimbish

Hospital in Winfield, Kansas. This was in the Fall of 1957. After the 29 days in the hospital, the leg was in a cast for about 2 months. He had to use crutches to get around, and had to elevate the leg while sitting at his school desk. We were loaned a hospital bed during this time, so that he could also elevate the leg at home.

The doctor, a Dr. Young, I believe the name was, had said that the infection could only be removed by scraping the bone. Since the infection was situated in the growing end of the bone, the scraping of that portion of the bone made it unlikely that the bone would

Johnny Plowboy

continue to grow normally. The result would be a left leg shorter than the other—not a happy prospect for an active boy who loved baseball.

We prayed, and our whole church joined in prayer. We at that time attended First Assembly of God in Mulvane, Kansas, pastored by Rev. J. C. Hinds. As Ken grew, it became apparent that the left leg was keeping pace with the other, and growing normally. He grew to over six feet tall, and served in the Air Force. What a testimony to the healing power of prayer!

Loran D. Wimbish, with Ken Wimbish

CHAPTER TWENTY-THREE

I spent ten and a half years with the Boeing Airplane Company in Wichita, Kansas. During all that time, we held religious meetings every day at lunch time. All who wanted to come were welcome, from whatever church denomination. We had up to nine denominations represented in the meetings. A room was made available for us to meet in. On Mondays, we had verse-by-verse Bible study. On Wednesdays, we had prayer meeting. On Fridays, different ones from the group would

Johnny Plowboy

speak or give testimonies. On Tuesdays and Thursdays, we met in the open shop in an old-fashioned street-evangelism type meeting.

A number of men got saved and joined in with the group. Many of them gave testimony that they had been in church for years without realizing that they weren't saved. Some had even been workers in their churches, being Sunday school teachers and such, without ever being truly saved. In one such case, a fellow who was a Sunday school teacher in a church in Augusta, Kansas came to me one day and told me he wasn't saved. When I asked him what had brought him to that conclusion, he

Loran D. Wimbish, with Ken Wimbish

told me that it was the verse-by-verse Bible study that he had attended in that room in the Boeing Plant.

Another man had for years been a member of a large and fashionable church. Though his pastor had lots of theological training, this man hadn't realized that he was not saved. His testimony was that a fellow worker with no theological training led him to a real experience of salvation and personal relationship with the Lord.

One fellow saved there became a preacher, and went into full-time evangelistic work. Another entered the ministry,pioneering and

Johnny Plowboy

pastoring a church in which I have had the privilege of preaching. These are a few examples of what happened over a ten-year period.

One of the most outstanding things that took place was a conversion in one of our open-shop meetings. In that setting, there would be men eating lunch, talking, playing cards, even napping. In the case I will now relate, a young man sat at a table, just within earshot, playing cards. He appeared not to be paying any attention to us, but he couldn't turn a deaf ear to what was going on. He got up from the table, threw down his cards, and

Loran D. Wimbish, with Ken Wimbish

walked directly over to where we were. He boldly gave his heart to the Lord.

He eventually trained for missionary work. Years later, I had the privilege, while reading a missionary magazine, to read an article about him and his work in Brazil. Accompanying the article was a picture of him and his family. Imagine the pleasure of seeing him there—the same young man that had years before left his card game to follow Jesus.

I think of II Corinthians 9:10: "He who supplies seed to the sower, and bread for food, will supply and multiply the seed you have sown and increase the fruits of your

Johnny Plowboy

righteousness." When you supply seed for some sower, and he sows the seed, it becomes a crop, which is made into bread to eat, and which supplies seed for the next planting. So the Christian workers in those lunch-time meetings in the Boeing Aircraft plant, though they may not have gone to a foreign missionary field themselves, supplied seed to that boy who was saved there. He took that seed to Brazil, South America, and only eternity will reveal the results of that sowing.

Loran D. Wimbish, with Ken Wimbish

CHAPTER TWENTY-FOUR

I have always tried to be helpful to fellow workers. We have seen and known of encouraging results, but of course sometimes we would wonder, Did I do any good in that place? Sometimes, God would, after a while, slip back the curtain just a little and give us a glimpse of something encouraging.

One such case came from a period in our early married life. I was working in a factory in Fort Smith, Arkansas. Beside witnessing one on one to fellow workers, I would sometimes

Johnny Plowboy

approach a group of men and ask if I could read some scripture and speak to them. I always carried a New Testament in my pocket for that purpose. If the group was agreeable to that, I would read and speak, usually about salvation. I did not work at that place very long, and I did not see any obvious results from my ministry to the men.

Many years passed, and I was living in another state. Our family was on vacation, and, since we were away from home on a Sunday, we went to a church we of course had never been to. (I don't like to miss church even when I'm on vacation.) During Sunday school class,

Loran D. Wimbish, with Ken Wimbish

I saw a man that I recognized. He had worked in that factory in Fort Smith all those years ago. He had a Bible and some Sunday school literature in his hand.

Between Sunday school and the beginning of Morning Worship service, he saw me and recognized me. When he came over to shake hands, I said, "You weren't saved the last time I saw you."

"No," he said, "but do you remember when we worked together in Fort Smith? You were always reading your New Testament and preaching at lunch time. I never did get away

Johnny Plowboy

from that; it eventually brought me to the Lord".

I asked, "Who is the pastor here?"

"I am," he responded, "and you are preaching for me this morning." The Lord blessed, and we had a wonderful time of getting reacquainted and of fellowshipping together.

Loran D. Wimbish, with Ken Wimbish

CHAPTER TWENTY-FIVE

I believe that God has always had His hand upon me, and guided me. As I look back, I can see His hand very clearly in my life. It seems that most of His guidance has been by circumstances, but even so, His hand was there through it all.

A few times, I have been able to get definite direction from the Lord just by asking. One such time was in 1957. I had been working in a machine shop in Tulsa, Oklahoma, for a company that also had a shop in Pampa, Texas.

Johnny Plowboy

When they closed the Tulsa shop and moved it's operations to Texas, they offered to take on the Tulsa employees at the Pampa shop. I don't recall that any employees went there, except for some management personnel.

At that time, the Boeing Airplane Company in Wichita, Kansas had a representative in Tulsa who was looking for machinists. Four of us talked with him, all four were hired, and we all went to work in Wichita.

Boeing hired and laid off according to what they called a "forecast", which seemed to come almost daily. We had been there only a few weeks when our foreman told us that a lay-off

Loran D. Wimbish, with Ken Wimbish

was coming on Friday of that week. Since we were the last hired, we could expect to be the first to go. We had not even as yet served out our probationary period.

The four of us from Tulsa got together and talked about the matter. We decided to call our former company and see if their offer was still good to hire us at the Pampa shop.

It occurred to me that I had just made the decision on my own, and had not asked the Lord what to do, so I confessed to the Lord my wrong, and asked what He wanted me to do. He promptly replied that I should stay put at Boeing. I told the other fellows that I had

Johnny Plowboy

changed my mind, and would not be going to Texas. They thought it foolish of me, but I acted on what I was sure the Lord wanted. They left immediately.

Before Friday came and they distributed the lay-off notices, one man who worked there said, "The lay-off will stop at that fellow Wimbish; they will not lay him off." When someone asked him why he believed that, he said, "Because he is a man who trusts in the Lord, and God will take care of him."

Sure enough, when they come around on Friday with the lay-off notices, they came down to me and stopped there. I was not laid

Loran D. Wimbish, with Ken Wimbish

off, and I remained employed there for just over ten and one-half years. I became involved with the group of Christian workers that I mentioned earlier. We spent our lunch hours every day of the week in the gospel meetings that I have described already—this during the whole time that I was there. I have sometimes said that I doubt that there is an industrial plant in the nation that has had more gospel bounced off it's walls than that old Boeing Aircraft plant in Wichita, Kansas.

Boeing built the B-52 bomber. When they finished that contract, they did not get another major contract at that time. Thousands of

Johnny Plowboy

people were let out of work. There were not enough jobs around Wichita to absorb all the laid-off workers.

I found out that there were opportunities for skilled machinists in the Phoenix area. I made contact there, and was assured that I would be welcome. I planned to leave for Phoenix in two weeks, all the while seeking God to know what His plans were for me. As the two weeks were passing by, I noticed an advertisement in the Wichita paper by a Joplin, Missouri company that was looking for machinists. I checked with that company, and they hired me, so we came this way. That was almost thirty years ago.

Loran D. Wimbish, with Ken Wimbish

I can see very clearly the hand of God in all of that. Had I gone to Phoenix, I am sure I would have spent the rest of my life in the West. But God brought me here, to Southwest Missouri. I have met some precious and wonderful people here. Last night, as we sat in our Wednesday night church service, I thought of all the ways that God has led me throughout my life. As I reflected on His guidance, I was convinced that He had placed me where I was sitting at that moment. I was there among people that I have grown to love and appreciate, people that have meant so much to me in the past few years.

Johnny Plowboy

Of course, if I had not met them here I would have met them in Heaven. But since it was my privilege to get acquainted with them here, we won't have to make acquaintance over there. We will just join together and begin our eternal praise and worship of our wonderful Lord, and have fellowship together.

Glory, Hallelujah, Praise the Lord! I'll meet you there!

Loran D. Wimbish, with Ken Wimbish

Epilogue

I personally lived through some of the events described in these pages, and know them to be true accounts of things that happened to my dad and to our family. It has been my great good fortune to write into a book these stirring and faith-strengthening stories, which has been done to uplift the reader and to glorify God.

Many of the events that are written about here occurred before my birth in 1946. It has been a joy for me to record these along with

Johnny Plowboy

the ones I do remember. Some of the stories I have heard my dad relate from the pulpit on numerous occasions, and God used them in a powerful way to work mightily in the lives of the hearers. May it be so that they will once again, and repeatedly, be used to inspire hope and faith in many hearts.

My favorite story of healing, as you might guess, is the one that I myself experienced in 1958; it is recounted in Chapter Twenty-Two. I still get a thrill when I realize that God did a wonderful thing for me, when the doctors confessed that they could do nothing. Although that happened forty-four years ago, the

Loran D. Wimbish, with Ken Wimbish

memory is still fresh and stimulating, and a daily source of joy and awe to me.

May each and every reader come to a greater realization of God's love and power, and to a greater commitment to follow Him Whom to know is life eternal.

—Ken Wimbish

About the Author

Loran Daniel Wimbish

Loran D. Wimbish is a former pastor, evangelist and bible teacher. He spent over fifty years as a machinist, working for Douglas in Tulsa and Boeing in Wichita, serving all the while the church of his beloved Lord. He has resided in the same home in Southwest Missouri for over twenty-seven years, along with his wife of fifty-nine years, Mary Nadine Manning Wimbish. He has four children, six grandchildren and a great-granddaughter.

Kenneth Wayne Wimbish

Ken Wimbish had a long career as a professional guitarist and singer. He is now a disc jockey and radio announcer. After many years in California, Ken now happily resides in Southwest Missouri. He has one daughter, one son and one granddaughter.

Printed in the United States
904500001B